SOMERS LIBRARY

# EUGENE

# JAMES MARSHALL

**HOUGHTON MIFFLIN COMPANY BOSTON**

SOMERS LIBRARY

Copyright © 1975 by James Marshall

All rights reserved. For information about permission to
reproduce selections from this book, write to Permissions,
Houghton Mifflin Company, 215 Park Avenue South,
New York, New York 10003.

www.hmco.com/trade

Library of Congress Catalog Card Number: 00132436
ISBN 0-618-07319-1

Manufactured in the Singapore
TWP 10 9 8 7 6 5 4 3 2 1

Eugene was so excited. He could barely
finish his oatmeal. Summer was finally over,
and it was time for school to begin.

In the front hall Eugene paused to adjust his ear muffs. It was so important to make a good impression.

On the front steps he paused again, to check his satchel. Everything was there: two brand new pencils, a new box of Crayolas, and a brand new tablet.

On the way Eugene sang his very favorite

song. It was called "School Days."

But all of a sudden, something made him

stop singing. Someone nearby was making

an awful fuss.

"Oh dear me! Help, help!" squealed

a lady's voice.

He knocked on the door of the house where
the sound was coming from. "Come in quick!"
exclaimed the voice.

He opened the door and saw a lady in distress.
"Step on it, step on it before it gets me!"
squealed the lady.

"It's only a harmless little thing,"
said Eugene. "You mustn't be afraid."
"Oh, I'm so ashamed," said the lady.

Eugene had plenty of time before school, and he accepted the lady's invitation to join her for a plate of delicious buckwheat pancakes. Her breakfast nook was very cozy.

"May I give you a lift?" said the lady, stepping into her small roadster.

"No thank you," said Eugene, "I prefer to walk."

"Very well," said the nice lady. "I'm sure we'll meet again. Ta-ta, and thanks for everything. Next time I won't be afraid."

Eugene continued on his way. He was very happy to have been of service to the nice lady. In front of the school, he ran into some of his neighborhood friends. "Wipe that smile off your face, Eugene," they said. "All the older kids say that our teacher Miss Baxter is a real meanie."

Suddenly Eugene became very concerned.

"A real meanie," he thought to himself, "oh dear."

Eugene tried to imagine what Miss Baxter would look like. He imagined her looking very cross indeed.

"Golly," he thought, "maybe school isn't going to be so much fun as I had hoped."

When the school bell rang, Eugene felt all

funny inside.

Ever so slowly he peeked into the classroom.

And who do you suppose he saw sitting at

the teacher's desk?

Miss Baxter gave Eugene a big wink.

Eugene gave Miss Baxter a big wink too.

"School *is* going to be fun," he thought
to himself.

James Marshall, the creator of many hilarious books for children, including *Miss Nelson Is Missing* and *The Stupids Step Out,* has no rival when it comes to goofy fun. Filled with the same silly spirit and charm, his *Four Little Troubles* provide cozy comfort to young readers facing the universal troubles of childhood.

The *Four Little Troubles* series includes:
*Eugene*
*Sing Out, Irene*
*Snake: His Story*
*Someone Is Talking about Hortense,* written by Laurette Murdock

JP

MARSHALL, JAMES
Eugene

| | DATE DUE | | NOV 23 |
|---|---|---|---|
| OCT 28 2000 | | | |
| NOV 24 2000 | | | |
| Oct 22 | | | |
| | | | |
| | | | |
| | | | |
| | | | |
| | | | |
| | | | |
| | | | |

SOMERS LIBRARY